Reader's Clubhouse

LAN'S PLANT

By Sandy Riggs
Illustrated by Bob Masheris

BARRON'S

Table of Contents

Illustrations on pages 21 and 23 created by Carol Stutz

All inquiries should be addressed to:
Barron's Educational Series, Inc.
250 Wireless Boulevard
Hauppauge, New York 11788
www.barronseduc.com

Library of Congress Catalog Card No.: 2005053587

ISBN-13: 978-0-7641-3287-2
ISBN-10: 0-7641-3287-3

Library of Congress Cataloging-in-Publication Data
Riggs, Sandy, 1940–
    Lan's plant / Sandy Riggs.
       p. cm. – (Reader's clubhouse)
    ISBN-13: 978-0-7641-3287-2
    ISBN-10: 0-7641-3287-3
    1. Plants—Juvenile literature. 2. Prickly pears—Juvenile literature. I. Title.
II. Series.

QK49.R534 2006
580—dc22

                                                                2005053587

PRINTED IN CHINA
9 8 7 6 5 4 3 2 1

Dear Parent and Educator,

Welcome to the Barron's Reader's Clubhouse, a series of books that provide a phonics approach to reading.

Phonics is the relationship between letters and sounds. It is a system that teaches children that letters have specific sounds. Level 1 books introduce the short-vowel sounds. Level 2 books progress to the long-vowel sounds. This progression matches how phonics is taught in many classrooms.

Lan's Plant reviews the short "a" and "e" sounds introduced in previous Level 1 books. Simple words with these short-vowel sounds are called **decodable words.** The child knows how to sound out these words because he or she has learned the sounds they include. This story also contains **high-frequency words.** These are common, everyday words that the child learns to read by sight. High-frequency words help ensure fluency and comprehension. **Challenging words** go a little beyond the reading level. The child will identify these words with help from the illustration on the page. All words are listed by their category on page 24.

Here are some coaching and prompting statements you can use to help a young reader read *Lan's Plant:*

- **On page 4, "Lan" is a decodable word. Point to the word and say:**

  Read this word. How did you know the word? What sound(s) did it make?

  Note: There are many opportunities to repeat the above instruction throughout the book.

- **On page 5, the words "Lan" and "plant" have the same short-vowel sound "a."**

  Say: *Find and read two words on this page that have the same short-vowel sound. What short-vowel sound do they make? How did you know?*

You'll find more coaching ideas on the Reader's Clubhouse Web site: *www.barronsclubhouse.com.* Reader's Clubhouse is designed to teach and reinforce reading skills in a fun way. We hope you enjoy helping children discover their love of reading!

Sincerely,

Nancy Harris

Nancy Harris
Reading Consultant

Lan has a plant.

Lan likes her plant.

Her plant sits on a desk.

Her plant sits in the sun.

Sand is in the pot.

The sand is not wet.

Lan makes the sand damp.

Lan likes her plant.

Now the stems are fat
and flat.

Lan looks at her plant.

Lan sees a bug. It is a pest.

Go away, bad bug.

Now Lan has a big plant.

Her plant has a red bud.

Lan has the best plant.

Fun Facts About 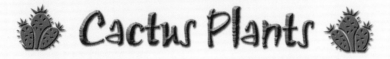 Cactus Plants

- Lan's plant is a prickly pear cactus. Although its flat pads look like leaves, they are called *stems.*

- Some wild animals eat prickly pear cactus for water and food. Cows also make a meal of these pads—once the ranchers remove the spines!

- The flower that appears at the tip of the cactus grows into a delicious red fruit. Prickly pear cactus can also be made into candy, syrup, jelly, and juice.

- A prickly pear cactus can range in height from 6 inches (15 centimeters) to 7 feet (2 meters).

- Here are some parts of the prickly pear plant:

fruit

spines

flower

stem

Make a Prickly Plant

You can make a cactus plant *almost* like Lan's.

You will need:
- brown clay
- green clay
- small paper cup
- toothpicks
- red paper
- pencil
- safety scissors
- glue

(Note to adult: Help children break toothpicks and supervise as they use them.)

1. Fill the cup with brown clay. This will be the pot of dirt for your plant.

2. Use the green clay to make fat, flat stems for your plant.

3. Break a few toothpicks into little pieces to make spines. Put them in the stems.

4. Place a long toothpick in the bottom of each stem.

5. Push the stems into the clay in the cup. Place them as close together as you can so they look like Lan's plant.

6. Draw a flower on the red paper and cut it out.

7. Glue the flower to your plant.

Word List

Short-A and Short-E Decodable Words	bad best damp desk fat	flat has Lan pest plant	sand stems wet
High-Frequency Words	a and are at away big go her in is it likes looks makes not now	on red sees the	